BEAR IN SUNSHINE

Written by Stella Blackstone
Illustrated by Debbie Harter

Barefoot Books
step inside a story

Bear likes to play
when the sun shines,

Bear likes to sing in the rain.

He flies his red kite
when the wind blows,

When it's icy,
he skates in the lane.

Bear likes to paint when it's misty,

When storms come, he hides in his bed.

When snow falls,
he likes to make snow-bears,

When the moon shines
he stands on his head.

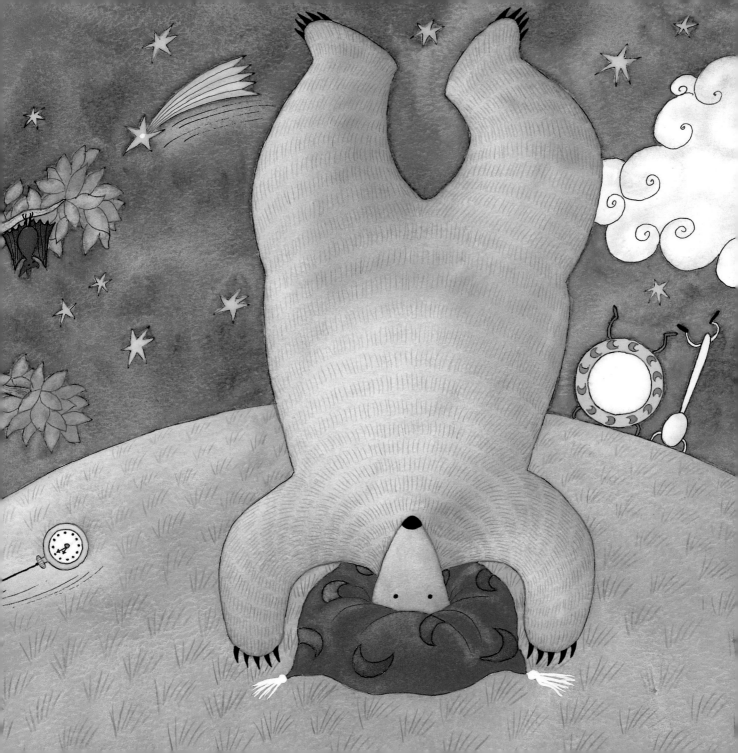

Bear always knows how to have lots of fun!

Spring

Summer

For more fun with Bear:

BEAR IN A SQUARE
Stella Blackstone
Debbie Harter

BEAR ON A BIKE
Stella Blackstone
Debbie Harter

BEAR'S BUSY FAMILY
Stella Blackstone
Debbie Harter

BEAR ABOUT TOWN
Stella Blackstone
Debbie Harter

BEAR TAKES A TRIP
Stella Blackstone
Debbie Harter

BEAR AT HOME
Stella Blackstone
Debbie Harter

BEAR AT WORK
Stella Blackstone
Debbie Harter

BEAR'S BIRTHDAY
Stella Blackstone
Debbie Harter

For Felix — S. B.
For Julia and Isabella — D. H.

Barefoot Books, 2067 Massachusetts Ave, Cambridge, MA 02140
Barefoot Books, 29/30 Fitzroy Square, London, W1T 6LQ

Text copyright © 2001 by Stella Blackstone
Illustrations copyright © 2001 by Debbie Harter
The moral rights of Stella Blackstone and Debbie Harter have been asserted

First published in the United States of America by Barefoot Books, Inc
and in Great Britain by Barefoot Books, Ltd in 2001
This paperback edition first published in 2019
All rights reserved

Graphic design by Polka. Creation, Bath
Reproduction by Grafiscan, Verona
Printed in China on 100% acid-free paper

This book was typeset in Slappy and Futura
The illustrations were prepared in paint,
pen and ink, and crayon

ISBN 978-1-78285-987-1

British Cataloguing-in-Publication Data:
a catalogue record for this book is available from the British Library
Library of Congress Cataloging-in-Publication Data
under LCCN 00012440

57986